STAR AND THE MYSTERY
OF THE MISSING CLOTHES

By Michael C. F. Cresswell

Dedicated to the endless possibilities of your imagination

THIS BOOK BELONGS TO

_____

_____

One marvellous day on the farm, in March,
a girl named Star had her birthday.

It was time to open her present. For her birthday, Star got a big, golden eagle! After she took the eagle out of the box, she trained it to not hurt anyone and land on her arm!

Star had to do her laundry. She took her clothes out to the brown river to hang them up with her golden eagle.

The eagle learnt to hang clothes on the clothes line and take them off when they are dry.

When Star and the golden eagle came back, they found
a crocodile dancing around with her clothes on!
Star and the golden eagle could not believe their eyes!

After they had a cup of tea and a cookie,
they went out to hang the washing
by the pig shed.

One hour later, Star came back to get her clothes. She could not believe it… this time, she saw the crocodile and a pig dancing with her clothes on!

She could not believe what she saw!
The crocodile! The pig! And a sheep!
All dancing around with her clothes on!

Star had enough of losing her clothes. She decided to put the last of her washing up in the house.
"I will hang them here, so the animals won't get them and dance around with them!" said Star.

But when she came back later, her clothes had all disappeared!
"Oh no! Where have all my clothes gone?" said Star.

Suddenly, Star heard some noise coming from outside.
She went out the front door to find…

All the animals were having a party!
All dancing around, all wearing Star's clothes!

THE EAGLE

THE RABBIT!

THE CROCODILE!

THE SHEEP!

THE CAT!

THE PIG!

Star was surprised but not upset.
Star laughed and laughed.

She then joined in the dancing and
fun with all the animals.

THE END

ABOUT THE AUTHOR

MICHAEL CRESSWELL

Born from the rainforest along the Great Barrier Reef on Yidinji country in a land called Oz. Michael has been an international teacher, leader and creator of schools spanning eight countries and three continents. The stories, love and passion for teaching children and educators around the world has provided the imagination for publishing children's books. He is a past Australian national basketball champion and currently resides in Scarborough, UK and Lago di Como, Italia with Alice and a Sicilian street dog called James.

There are more stories to come!

Printed in Great Britain
by Amazon

32915294R00016